Walter Noetico
Diderot's Dream

For the 300th birth anniversary

FOREWORD

By means of honouring the memory of Denis Diderot on the occasion of the third centenary of his birth in 2013, I wished to present this short novel, as if this was his unpublished manuscript which was discovered today, accompanied by a letter sent to his beloved Sophie Volland, wherein Diderot retells his dream.

The letter is dated Paris, 20th September 1769, few days after Diderot actually wrote his work entitled: "The Dream of d'Alembert".

With this imaginary literary discovery, I desired to bring back to life the contemporaneity of the eternal universality of thought of the great philosopher.

Walter Noetico

Letter from Denis Diderot to Sophie Volland

Paris, 20th September 1769

My good friend, in my last letter of 11th of September, I had written that I have completed the Dream of d'Alembert, and what would have made you amazed is that the Dream of d'Alembert appears to be against religion, notwithstanding that there had been no word on religion.

But what will amaze you even more, my beloved Sophie, is that I really did have a dream that this time speaks above all of religion. Perhaps because my voluntary tether, which prevented me from talking about religion in the Dream of d'Alembert, broke, shattering into hundreds of pieces produced by a force that had accumulated and imprisoned for too long.

It took me more than seven days to transcribe in detail this dream, which is even more insane and, therefore, I hope it is wiser than the one invented for d'Alembert. In this oneiric vision, I am as if projected in time, equally in the past and in the future, and even in space, because the places where I find myself are always different.

Then there are many unique characters, and what happens is even more remarkable, such as Jesus Christ who returns to earth after 2013 years, thus in the future when I shall have exactly 300 years.

I do not understand why my dream is gone into the future; I hope it is a prophetic dream and that 2013 marks the beginning of the end of the Christian era.

It is very strange that I dream of Christ, whose reality - as you know – I do not even acknowledge, because there exists no testimony of neither of the several historians of his time on his extraordinary and miraculous existence, as asserts also my friend Voltaire. Certainly, I dreamed of Christ because the doctrine of this literary character for centuries governs our time and the consciousness of mankind.

It appears truly that in this dream there is a state of eternity, because its protagonists are still alive even after thousands of years, and this dream has its beginning in 313 in Milan with the Emperor Constantine I, as he pronounces his edict which legalised the Christian religion, and consequently the beginning of power of the Church throughout the Roman Empire. Even though it is actually in 380 with the Edict of Thessalonica, issued by Theodosius and signed by the emperors Gratian and Valentinian II, that Christianity becomes the official religion of the Empire, strictly forbidding all religious cults related to the ancient mythological divinity.

However, without the support of Constantine I, who proclaimed very resolute laws in favour of the Christians, the Church would not have had the power it has subsequently had throughout the Roman Empire. Certainly, his favour towards the Christians was originated by the influence of his mother

Helen, who also built two churches, and the clergy proclaimed her a saint, and also because the Christian God was the only one who could forgive him the killing of his wife Fausta and his son Crispus.

It also seems to me quite strange that I was born exactly 1400 years after Constantine's edict.

You are aware of how rational is my mind, and how I have always refused any discipline such as numerology, astrology or other illogical things of this kind, however I must admit that the geometry had always surprised me, together with a certain aesthetic rule of nature, such as, for example, during the cold winters, when the ice crystals are formed on the window glass; always so new and different depending on the moisture and temperature of the air, as to excite a mathematician such as d'Alembert.

It appears as though the nature has in itself the order of all things, and not all is made so incidentally.

The key character of this dream is a woman called Christiana, and is undoubtedly the symbol of Christianity. I, however, appear in the dream - what I had always dreamed of being: man of the Liberation, an anti-Redeemer, even though I have the same age and the likeness of Christ. It will be because I recognize in this character my own aspirations: those to improve the human-being.

It will be appreciated if you read all of the dream that I have written in the pages annexed herewith, so that you will get a clearer idea of what I am telling.

I divided the dream in scene chapters, as if all is taking place in a theatre.

I am very anxious to learn of your opinion, when you have finished reading it, although I am pleased to anticipate that this dreamlike fantasy is liable to go to the stake fire. For this reason, I ask you kindly to preserve this letter and manuscript in a hidden place. Here where I am, there is always a risk that the police can do a search.

Farewell my tender friend, if this dream will make your hair stand, please do not blame me. In truth, what exists better than to stay with you and open up all of my heart? Farewell, farewell.

DREAM'S DIDEROT

CHARACTERS:

Christiana : "Symbol of Christianity and spirituality of Man"

The Master : "Jesus Christ"

The Man of Liberation : "Denis Diderot"

The Poverello : "Saint Francis of Assisi "

Caesar : "Symbol of Power"

Peter : "The Apostle founder of the Church "

Monsignor Pastor : "The symbol of the spiritual decadence"

Scene No. 1

Roman Epoch.

313 A.D. Constantine I, delivers his edict which legalized the Christian religion, in the arena of Milan full of people, and encourages his subjects to embrace Christianity.

Scene No. 2

In the gallery of a luxurious patrician villa.

Christiana, a beautiful young woman is standing and admiring with an amiable expression the marble busts and portraits in mosaic on the walls of her thirty-three ancestors, from St. Peter to Pope St. Sylvester I, arranged in order of succession.

It is a beautiful spring morning, the sun beams come through the windows illuminating the gallery.

While the woman is admiring the recent

marble bust of San Silvestro, she realizes that the clothes she wears constantly change their appearance, according to the fashion of different eras until 2013. In gallery too, all the mosaics and marble busts which depict her ancestors, are enriched with two hundred and fifty other portraits of various popes until 2013.

The gallery itself also changes its appearance and the Roman villa transforms itself into a white Palladian villa, surrounded by a park next to a hill, above which there is an enormous sphere of light.

Scene No. 3

Christiana comes out appalled and frightened from the gallery, opening a door to the garden and moves running toward the sphere of light on the nearby hill.

Having arrived at the foot of the sphere, she sits on the ground, exhausted, breathless, with a disturbed expression on her face.

Few seconds later, still on the ground, she raises her eyes to the sphere and sees - in the midst of a strong light - the figure of a young man of about thirty, with no clothes on, and who is busy working on the sphere.

- What are you doing? - she asks him, still panting.

- Do you not see? - replies the man without looking at her, scraping away the trappings of the Liberation.

- And what about you, who are you? - and why have you no clothes on?

- I am the Man of the Liberation, I do not need clothes.

- How strange, I have never seen before that thing on which you are working ...

- And now you see it?

- I just cannot see anything, I cannot distinguish anything, there is too much light, too much fog, where does it all come from?

- It is here, it has always been!

- Do you work for someone?

- No. - replied the man looking at her,

- Why do you work then?!

- Because it is my duty to do so.

- But later, whom will you tell of the Liberation?

- No one.
- In this way, no one would be able to see it, - she murmurs regretfully. How long will it take for you to complete the work?

- All the time I have left.

- But is it not yours, the Lliberation?

- In fact, it belongs to all free men.

- If you reveal the discovery, you would become very famous.

- I do not barter Freedom with popularity. - says the man vigorously - nor will I feed the jaws of cultural speculation.

- Then I do not think that someone will pay you for this work of yours ...

- I know. – says the man with a smile.

- And it does not matter to you? Why do you do it then?

- Just as a testimony for those who will find it – replies the man.

   - And why? - adds Christiana – Do you love so much the Freedom?

   - Everyone loves very much the Freedom, although not everyone can pay the tribute it requires.

   - Freedom, - he adds - a word that lends itself to be quite a lot misinterpreted.

- What do you say! - she says arrogantly - Freedom means choosing.

- The only possible Freedom is in the consciousness of Truth. - replied the man.

- But I am Christiana and I am the Truth!

- Instead, I believe that it is solely the freedom of thought that carries you to the Truth, and I am convinced that the moral integrity derrives solely from an individual search of the Truth. Only in this way, man will reach the Freedom.

Scene No. 4

In the little church of the villa, the bells are ringing. Some of the faithful believers are preparing to enter the church.

Christiana is still sitting on the floor next to the man and the sphere of light. She rises up and tidies the dress.

- Now I have to go to church. - she says calmly, - Why do not you get dressed and join me too? Today is the day of Easter!

- I am not a believer. - replied the man.

- Shall I find you here afterwards? - She adds.

As she utters this last phrase, he notices that the two men are approaching her. One man is wearing a rumpled tunic together with a mantle coat all frayed and held askew over one shoulder, with an untidy beard and his black hair all disheveled.

The other man, of a smaller stature, is walking a step behind the other, wearing a robe and his hands folded in the sleeves. His face is thin, pale and glabrous, with quiet and resigned expression.

- Have you seen?! - she whispers to the Man of Liberation with the withered voice in the throat.

- They have arrived - the Master and the

Poverello. – utters she with tremulously.

- Yes, I saw, I know. – says the man, turning towards the two men who are staring at him without any surprise.

The Man and the Master have identical faces as if they were identical twins, the only difference is in the beard of the Master.

- We finally arrived! - Master sighs heavily.

The two men sit themselves on the floor at the foot of the sphere of light.

- Two thousand years I am waiting for this moment. – says the Master with a slight smile on his lips, to the Man of Liberation.

- What year is it now?

- We are in 2013 after your event, nathurally. - The man replies.

- You know, - continues the Master always looking at the man – there, from where I come from, two thousand years ago everyone was expecting a Messiah for many centuries. Even the populace was saying that certain ancient prophets have announced it, so I thought ... - says absorbed and circumspect - why cannot I be the Messiah? .. Well, I was taken by one of those spasmodic fevers that I cannot even find the words to describe! I pondered and pondered long on the situation and gradually began to put myself into the part, all the way! It was so exciting! Mind you, it was not a joke to assume the role of the savior, there was a life at risk! Of course it was, I was full of enthusiasm and inevitably I ended up blindly believing it myself! Blindly, - repeats the Master emphatically and continues: - I believed in my mission, and then you know how it is, when we are young, we are a bit insane, and sometimes you want to overdo matters. However, I dreamed of something really great that would take me away from mediocrity ... Already then, there was no more escape. – he muttered discouraged – one need to try always... at times one also comes across the frustrations ... I have never had the father ... but I was sincere! And now?

- With the coercion of the human spirit you have furnished the great assumptions to the power – says the man with a slight reproach, while continuing his work - Was not this what you wanted? You said that those who do not believe in you will not have eternal life, so for better or worse they have adapted.

- Not you though! – responds the Master in a haste and appears strange as he utters this, and it is not clear whether he feels joy or anger.

The man then smiles a little to himself.

- Moreoever, all of them are lies! - continues the Master harshly - You know better than me that it is nonsense, - adds less violently - they have invented many stories after my death, I swelled up like a balloon thereafter! First they murder you, and after make you rise again. It always happens this way, always so happens that in the beginning you are not understood, and much less probable that you are accepted, and certainly they do not seek to discuss your ideas, and much less appreciate what might be useful to the common progress! What they fear is the uprising of the people, they see ghosts of revolution everywhere, thus they kill you and create a fetish of the martyr! Thereafter, you are dumped as food at the new generations with the good and bad, so that no one will dare challenge you: you are now God! ... Finally, all is well seasoned with various sauces such as miracles ... And there you have the super lollipop for the people.

Christiana gazes at the Master shocked and dazed, shortly after she faints.

Scene No. 5

In the Palladian Villa

It is evening, the villa and the park are lit. Inside the villa, there is a masquerade party, many guests wear costumes of the various epochs of human history, from two thousand years ago until the present day.

Christiana is wearing Roman dress and is dancing with a man dressed as Caesar, who has the same appearance of Constantine I. The two are obviously in love.

The ballroom and the whole house are decorated in the style of Louis XVI, so are also the clothes of the musicians of the orchestra.

- Do you love me, my love? – says she enraptured.

- Could I not? - replies the man dressed as Caesar, - You are so beautiful and desirable. - says running his fingers over her mouth, and slowly on the neck, - I shall always love you, and you?

- You know that first will cease the life. – she murmurs with emotion - What do you think, will it be beautiful our life?

- Wonderful, my love, it will be wonderful. - says the man dressed as Caesar, kissing her neck.

- It is a wonder to stay together forever? It is so sweet to sleep together, wake up and find ourselves one beside the other every morning, every moment of the night, every day, every thousand moments ...

The Minuet that was danced ends.

A large reception, - he says - a really marvellous evening, - and taking her hand he adds, - come on let us go to the buffet, are you not hungry?

The two move towards the buffet, smiling and happy.

- You know, - she says turning suddenly serious - that there are two categories of men? Those who are free and those who are not.

- What does it matter to us! – pretending not to see anything, taking a tart from the tray - Here we have plenty of bread, look at that splendid buffet, it is truly wonderful.

She looks around uneasily, awaiting his evasive answer. And thus she captures the disease at fault, a strange and monstrous figure with two humps, one on the chest and the other on the back, with a face full of buboes, leaps into the guest room among the unsuspecting guests. And as he passes by their side, the faces and hands of the guests turn white with blue spots and red swellings.

- We have to get out in the air!!! – she screams terrified.

- Do you want the salmon mousse? - he says, smiling, full of buboes.

Scene N° 6

Rome: The Cathedral of San Pietro

We are always in the spring, the sky is threatened by an unusual storm.

Christiana is sitting on the steps of the altar

in the center of the ciborium by Bernini. The Cathedral is deserted, next to her sits the Apostle Peter dressed in a style of two thousand years ago.

- You see Christiana, - says Peter with patronizing tone, - I have not searched for the reasons in not believing in God, not only for the fact that the Church disappointed me. This would have been too simplistic, a kind of psychological vindication, do you understand? As it happens to those who somehow feel so tried and mistreated by God, to be induced to deny their existence. In short, a revenge. And in my mind there ignited small fires. This idea tortured and obsessed me for a long time, and one day I said to myself: "How can I talk to others about God with such an absolute certainty, when mine is faltering?

That is why I left the Church, I was no longer at ease ... I seemed indeed to support an arbitrary role. I, in my condition as a Vicar of God, felt guilty; I thought that this condition should take place and prosper solely on a matter of conscience as is religion, indeed! I realized that it is a case of collective consciousness, God himself is a case of conscience. And you know what? I can say with this, to have given a name to all of my questions.

Christiana, with the facial expression of surprise and sorrow, stares at Peter with eyes wide open. The sky has darkened.

- You see, - continues Peter, - I have often asked myself why we humans must accept categorically all sorts of limitations and inhibitions precisely above all the fundamental themes of existence. I think that in this case, God himself would fallen into contradiction: having created the animal-man with a brain so advanced and unique, and then prevented it from being used for his conquests of knowledge?

- Peter! Will there be a solution? – asks she.

- Well, - answers Peter, emerging from a long silence, - I think it will be very difficult and painful, like a flaying of the skin. In a certain sense it is much more comforting to succumb to the idea of God, as if falling a prey to a small fever with which one can exist without problems.

- But you are Peter! - exclaims the woman with a air of rebellion, - Do you remember what the Master said: "and on this rock I shall build my Church."

- Of course I am Peter, but since then had passed two thousand years, and the Church which I founded is no longer the Church of Christ, from other 1600 years, from when the Church had become the official religion of the whole Roman Empire, and above all after the decrees of Theodosius in 391, when the Church has established itself with the most brutal violence against the people, with horrendous penalties of death and confiscation of assets of those who worshiped and recognized other deities.

The Master also said that one must leave Caesar's things to Caesar, however this had not occurred for the Church, because when it acquired the power it acted as would have behaved Caesar, eliminating all those who opposed to his law.

Apart from that, - continues Peter - my way of thinking now is different from what it was then; now I believe that the origin of all the living forms does not depend on the will of God, but from an evolutionary and eternal fact of the universe.

All of a sudden from the side of the basilica, come out the transparent figures of about 250 popes in the history of the Church, who wear the vestments of different historical periods. Everyone sings a liturgical hymn, occupying its place around the tabernacle, after a while the ciborium is all surrounded by popes. The first circle of popes around the twisted columns is suspended a few inches off the ground, the last circle being several meters higher. The circles are in a sloping scale, as a Roman amphitheater.

While the popes continue to sing, Peter rises up and goes to the center of the altar, turns and faces Christiana who is seated, and facing the Popes, he says with a certain fervor:

- You see, I do not want to eliminate the concept of God at all costs! ... But I want to be as objective and honest as possible, and then if we think well about it, what has our spirituality got to do with the coercive and capillary organisation of the Church? What can there be said about an entity that does not stand up to the judgement of deep self-analysis? And which sets down its roots and its domination in the inviolable mysteries?! In a process for plagiarism wihich impartial judge would accept as evidence the mystery? And in any case, by what right one can manipulate the present restlessness of man in front of certain unknown existential? Even if we must accept that the Church, through the spectacular choreography of its rites, largely achieves its scope. Nailed by the influence, we stand there helpless! But as soon as there is a will to reflect, inevitably we realize that all that they had given us is nothing more than a dismay of a permanent chrysalis . We did not have wings! – says Peter with eyes full of incredulity, and continues: - We had not the wings at all.

- Well. – continues Peter calmer, while the chorus of the popes is incessant, - If you want to give the name of God an existence, interpreted in his utter significance, then God is the nature, the man himself, the essence of his being, the universe, the love, the infinite, the eternal. In this case, it is another matter, it is a concept that goes well. However, it should not in any case be called God, because the meaning of God is above all the power over man, the government, condition, judgement, dependancy.

- And what one might call it? – asks she.

- I do not know in any way, I think. It does not matter … I think that the meaning of things is not in the things themselves and not in their name. In any way, if a man is fixed on the idea of God, if he believes or wants to believe at any cost and he really cannot do without it, I am of the opinion that he should do so in an individual form, private, away from the group degeneration and away from all those forms of external cult worship, where more than a real aspiration to authenticity, one finds in force the automatism of rules and ritualisms mainly connected to the hierarchy and politics.

The Popes continue to sing their liturgical hymn more vigorously. The storm rages, pours down a very heavy rain. Peter is always standing in the middle of the ciborium, with Christiana sitting opposite on the steps of the altar completely naked. Her expression and her posture are petrified and she looks at Peter with her eyes wide open.

No one cares about the rain. A strong light illuminates Christiana. Her joints are connected to the long string of a puppet.

- I do not support, - says Peter emphatically - that other men are much better and completely pure. - he says pointing his finger and looking at the popes. - However, at least …. at least they will not proliferate the name of God at every opportunity given! This chimeric God! - and then says heatedly – I am an individual who forms a part of these structures, like it or not! I am forced to see them, to support them to accept their effects, even if I do not wish! .... On the other hand, the times have changed and I cannot go around making justice on my own.

- And now, - says Christiana, with a worrying tone, - what will you do then?

- How will I do? ... I shall find a system, at least I shall try! ... At least for the sake of not being one of many, for whom it is enough to have a belly full and not to care about the human condition. I have to keep the sense of the universal things! Not like those living corpses that heat in vain their bench, weighing dead on the ground, hampering the path of man's intellectual and moral growth.

At this point, two popes who were behind his shoulders, descend down to the ground level of Peter and gently grab his arms. Peter tries to break free from the immaterial grip of the two, unsuccessfully, then begins shouting continuing his discourse: -

- Like an immense flock of sheep dumb and stupid, constructed of opportunism and lack of character, able only to be led by shepherds and their dogs, and which are ultimately sheared off the last lock of Will!

Peter ended speaking, the choir of pontiffs too end their singing, and Peter - between the two pontiffs transparent and intangible – also becomes transparent and intangible. After few seconds, all the pontiffs including Peter disappear. There remains only the young woman invaded by light, motionless and petrified with staring look on her face.

Scene N° 7

Towards the beginning of the 13th Century

In place of the Palladian villa there is now a castle. From the gate of a courtyard of the castle, leaves a procession led by a bishop sitted under a purple colour canopy supported by four prelates, followed by hooded men who are holding a half-naked man chained, who barely stands on his legs, and his body and face are tortured.

The place where emerges the luminous sphere, remains unchanged as an island out of time. The Man of Liberation, the Master, the Poverello (the poor man) and the young woman are at the foot of the sphere and are standing watching the procession with great interest. Christiana is wearing a dress in a style of the beginning of the 13th Century. The long procession stops in front of a pile of wood. The hooded men drag the chained man by force, place him on the pile of wood and then tie him up. The bishop blesses the man and then the fire is given to the wood.

- But what are they doing!? - exclaims shouting the Master.

- They are doing justice to the heretic! A traitor of the faith! Your traitor. – responds Christiana.

- Today, - she adds, - they sanctify your name and holy Easter with this sacrifice; today is being born the holy Inquisition which will last many centuries and protect the Church from heresy - concludes he with haughtiness.

- Madmen! Insane criminals! - shouts the Master, and after a few seconds adds,- Who thinks anymore to avenge the innocent dead? - says dismal Master - I have a throne, - cries the Master - that rises above endless piles of exterminated corpses! ... Underneath my throne, - cries even louder - there are more those murdered than martyrs! But surely for all of you, - pointing to the crowd – the corruption is obvious and irrelevant, quite natural.

- What do you say?! - says Christiana haughtily, - You do not realize that you are blaspheming; eliminating the heretics is a sacred task for the victory of your Church, for your victory.

- In truth I lost. With all honesty, for these your words that I lost! - Master says bitterly. - I have not yet understood what meaning give men to their lives. The stupid and the weak cling to illusions! ... The most evoluted are associated well enough with the system of power. All those who have something to lose or only a lethargy to preserve, heave and tremble at every blowing of the wind that brings an echo of innovation. Always the same story!

- Have you lost the sense of your doctrine?

- I tell you, that anyone who relies on whatever creed trasmitted and pre-existing to that actual one, with his own free self-search, relies upon a sterile and lethal faith.

- Master, - says Christiana boldly with haughtiness and resentment, - You are biased and in error, perhaps you need medical care, you cannot overturn the world, and what you taught us - you cannot destroy everything: the customs, morals, all our civilization.

- It seems to me that these teachings have failed to improve the man. On the contrary, it appears to me that they prevent him from giving his best, to be the best.

- Deny everything then, - she says with the harsh and reproachful voice.

- Certainly, my resurrection too and the resurrection of the flesh, - said the Master with carelessness. - They have invented it on purpose to make an impact upon the people who are backward and superstitious.

- Thou hast brought love and equality.

- Yes, look at that love! - shouts the Master angrily pointing at the one was being burned alive writhing in the flames of the stake. - Look what love, - he repeats, - But instead, I say to you, - continues a little calmer, - that I made up the dreams only for the underprivileged of life, and some I had put in the yoke, and others I had issued with the licence for the most total iniquity.

- Look at how you deceive thee, - she says - You have no more mental clarity! You must believe me because you are God and you are risen. If it were as you say, the others would have said so.

- Yes, - replicated the Master with mild irony, - Look at that poor chap, who had just had the audacity to challenge something! Now he is there, being burned.

Scene N° 8

Near the Luminous Sphere.

The Man of Liberation is standing and working on the sphere, from time to time his image disappears in the flickering light. The Master, the Poverello and Christiana are standing near the sphere. All three are watching a man dressed as a bishop, who precedes an enormous flock resembling a river whose banks are offset and swaying, where the black dogs with white collar are trying continously to re-embank the flock in a better way. The shepherd and the flock are going their way.

- Here is monsignor shepherd! – Christiana exclaims with joy, and looking at the Master. – He is one of your followers!

- Follower?! - Master says belligerently.

- You shall see, - steps in Christiana without minding his words, - he is very good and tender, and also very wise. He will dissuade you, you will see. He will convince you that you are wrong ... and will let you know how much powerful is your doctrine.

- Oh, I know! That what you call my doctrine, which then is not my true doctrine, - the Master says with a sneer of a bird of prey, - governs far and wide for two millennia! But what are the two thousand years in comparison to millions of years which remain for the earth and for man? Two thousand years are nothing! Provided that the man has not destroyed himself before then, and considering all that a man is and his deeds, the presumption is that it would have been very easy to do.

- Yes, of course, - he adds with disdain - and who would dream of denying the power of what you call my doctrine?! Its good submission is undisputed and indisputable. I am surprised, however, that every man is born with a brain formed in an unique way, independent and unrepeatable in nature. This is the only trace that leads us to its free origin, unconditional and random. You do not think about these things? - he says sarcastically. – Nonetheless, there had been on earth the philosophers and thinkers, but to what use is for a man to have an advanced intelligence, if he allows himself to be tethered without blinking as a beast of burden. How wrong I was. - says with desolation.

- No, not you, - she tells him eagerly. – You are not just anyone, you are God

- God, always God! – says the Master snorting impatiently. - Where is God? I have not ever seen him.

- What does it matter! You talk and talk, now you do not even know what you say.

- I speak for love, for truth I speak, - he says quite lost.

The pastor comes nearer to them, surrounded by the sheep who continues to bleat in its wobbly movements, and the dogs continue to bark trying to reorder them. The fat and ruddy pastor smiles benevolently to the three and raises his gloved and ringed hand to bless them.

- Oh, my Lord! - she whispers with the radiant face of joy. The Master makes two steps forward, livid in the face with the vein of the forehead that throbs. The Poverello,- he also approaches, with the eyes haggard and wet, and with reddened cheeks . The Man of Liberation does not pay attention to anything, indifferent and impassive, he continues his work on the sphere. The sheep continues to bleat in an increasingly intolerant way.

- Where are you going? – shouts the Master.

- Do you not see? - smiles at him the pastor with meekness, - I am taking the sheep to be sheared.

- It is not these sheep that I was talking about! – shouts the Master with ferocity.

- Why? - asks the annoyed shepherd - The wool yields well.

- And souls?

- It is all conglobated, is it not? – responds the shepherd laughing and amused.

- You, bastard! Disgusting bastard! Bastard leech. - cries the Master with more ferocity.

- What is the matter? Ugly beggar full of lice, how dare you. - the shepherd growls back at him - What do you want from me sacrilegious man? Get out of the way, let me pass, beggar!

 - Do you not recognize me anymore, eh? - Master says glowing – I, once again, have driven you away from the temple, mercenary impostors, cancer of humanity.

The pastor quivering raises his gold pastoral staff in order to hit the Master.

- Come here. – says the pastor between his teeth - Come closer if you dare! The stinking and dirty charlatan!

The Master, with the vein of the forehead increasingly red and swollen, loosens the belt of his robe to strike the pastor.

- Hold it! - says the Poverello (the poor man), holding him firmly by the arm.

- What is the Master for? - he says - As long as there are sheep, there will also be pastors.

- Are you scared, huh? - grins the pastor, still with pastoral staff being raised.

- Damn! - whispers the Master, bloodless white as dead.

- Go to hell! - the shepherd growls, recommencing his walk tidying up his robe.

Scene N° 9

Inside the white Palladian Villa.

Christiana is still terrified by the spread of the disease, which continues to wander among the unsuspecting guests who are now all infected and full of buboes, and who continue undisturbed their party. She searches with her eyes a way out, but as if paralysed, tries to move in order to escape, although her feet do not want to separate from the floor.

- My Love, - says the man dressed as Caesar - at least get some desert.

- I do not recognise you, - she says to him full of anger and terror - You have got to let me go.

- We love each other very much, - he says without listening what she had just said, filling up two glasses of champagne: - We toast to our happiness! – he exclaims handing to her the cup. She takes the cup against her will and calms down.

- What do you think of God and of religion? – asks then Christiana in a slight tone of irony and defiance.

- We are God and religion, - he replies smiling.

- We, - she says thoughtfully - Who knows what reality we live in, a reality that allows us the introspection.

- Come on dear, smile. - he says without minding her, dragging her into the circle of their guests. She looks at them and in everyone she sees the faces and hands full of bluish spots and buboes, all of whom smile at her and speak in an aphonic way.

- Who has the power is always loved. - says the man dressed as Caesar.

- But do you believe in God? – he asks Christiana.

- What importance is for us to believe; instead it is important that the people believe and it is this their faith that allows us to dominate them, and to exploit them to our liking. What matters is that they believe that we are sacred.

Scene N° 10

Always inside the white Palladian villa.

At the center of a large reception room, there is an enormous four-poster bed, around which there are four lit candles and funeral wreaths on the floor. Christiana is lying on the bed.

- I am dead. – she thinks from the bed, and sees herself with the agony that flips her eyes over, that she is ashen colour, with the grimace of death in the face.

- My Love, why do you not eat anything? - asks from the buffet the man dressed as Caesar, without losing his shine, except for patches of buboes.

- You are dead. - think of her the Man of Liberation, the Master and the Poverello, all of whom suddenly appeared in transparency around her bed.

- Here you are dead. - continue the three in pitiful acrimony.

- The Tribute! – she thinks again, - you have to pay the tribute. – she thinks;

- Am I dead? – with her eyes asks Christiana the Man of Liberation, full of despair, with a quiver of rebellion. – Am I dead? Am I dead? – she repeats in agony to the man of Liberation who is leant over the bed.

- Here is my desecration. They shall not understand and shall never accept it! And then, how could they? .. Their mind is like the water of a river that always flows into a river-bed with the banks too high, thus there is no deluge or current, and no innovator who will be able to bring it out. That water which is imprisoned by its own blind river banks. All men always create motives to justify their own outrage, to make them plausible! They call in for help the words such as love, affection, good, solidarity, safeguard of the welfare of others! ... With the kind words and the smiles they are seeking only to preserve intact their position ... They will never give up the exaggerated self-esteem to the position of one's ego ... Never will they see the symptoms of failure in their perfect construction! What does it mean to rebel? Perhaps it means just to seek the truth. Instead they unfairly transfer their primitive and fake instinct of preservation also to their children. They do not want the individual innovators! They just want perfect copies. – thinks Christiana.

The young woman looks around and sees, with an expression of terror, guests full of buboes, all of whom smile at her while approaching the bed from all sides. Man dressed as Caesar is already behind her and is sneering, holding tight those marionnette strings in his hand. He tries to move the joints of the woman, but is unable to, and then pulls stronger with anger, but the wires are tearing up in his hands. At the same moment, the guests, the guest room and everything that surrounds, slowly dissolves into nothingness.

Christiana attempts to cling to the Man of Liberation.

- Put me to safety! – she thinks, but it is like holding the air.

Scene N° 11

Rome, St. Peter's Square

Now Christiana and her bed are located in the center of the square, all crowded with numerous cathedrals of different architectural styles, the cathedrals are all golden and are splendidly shining in the sun. Christiana sits on the bed, looks at all around her with an expression of who has woken up after a long sleep; she has her eyes half-closed and dazzled by the glitter of the cathedrals. Suddenly, the sky obscrures almost completely, and she has the somewhat dismayed expression.

A silent rain descends upon the cathedrals in a withholding and cautious way, then becomes heavier and thunderous. The cathedrals are beginning to crumble under the heavy rain, becoming a mass of sludge.

The young woman is looking at the end of the cathedrals and large streams of mud and gold scrolling beside her. Thinks she:
-

- "As when you wake up after a long, very long slumber during which ideas and clichés, not necessarily our own and wishful, are entwined around us, weaving in abundance their dense branches on our motionless and passive state, up until it spreads its ramifications in an unique unbreakable matrix. It may happen that one day we discover that these tenacious and stubborn branches grow on our skin and on it proliferate as a kind of an immense lichen, which assimilates and greedily swallows every drop of our vitality, often weakening up to the point as to rout the pursuit of our identity." - after a few seconds she reflects again: - "Many of us upon awakening, now feel that the struggle is unequal. Many do not ever awaken and will never have any knowledge of themselves. Many more others take a glimpse and care less, satisfied with their reassuring squat. Some engage in the fight, but fall half way under their own shots of compromise.

Scene N° 12

Near the Luminous Sphere.

The man of Liberation is working suspended in mid-air on a surface of one side of the luminous sphere. The Master, the Poverello and Christiana are seated at the foot of the sphere. Their figures are surrounded by light.

- Master, - she says humbly with her eyes wide open – you have died in order to free us, to save us!

- There are many of those who have died for their ideas, over centuries, and they were not called God for this.

- But you are the one who had resurrected!

- Resurrected? To go where? - Says disdainfully with a harsh stare.

Christiana lowers her eyes for a few seconds, then gets a little aggressive.

- You told us so. – she says.

- Do you not see, - said the Master with a lot of pain – they have taken away the innocence!

- I pity all your tragic hope. - he says coldly, and after a few seconds of silence continues:

- Who knows why, - the Master says less coldly – it is easier to give to men a drink of lies, than the truth.

- But what have they done to you? - she exclaims prostrate – Do you not understand that you ought to believe, You yourself told us that we need to believe in someone! Faith is a force.

- And for this reason men will never be the protagonists of their lives. - Master says harshly.

- Now you want to take away from us everything? - says Christiana anxiously.

- Why do you not begin to believe in yourself? Poor puppets with loose strings. – says the Master with sadness.

- The faith is vital to us. - she says almost crying.

- Faith! – screams the Master all reddened with anger. – You speak of faith, but what faith?! The faith had become a museum piece, a sort of dusty archaeological find, your faith, a finding which you can show off on big occasions, like a phantasmagoria of illusions to be projected on a large desert scenery. After a few seconds of silence, the Master says calmly:

- Apart from him, him indeed! – says the Master pointing to the Poverello – He was really a mystic one; one of those rare exceptions in the history of the Church.

- The Poverello with his eyes wet and a slight smile looks at the Master and says: - Please do not flatter me, as it does not seem the case.

- Are you joking?! You were one of the few who have been consistent with my doctrine, in fact you were the best of all, and around you there has never been any shadow of falsehood or of iniquity!

- I did not even wear myself so much to do good. – says humbly the Poverello.

- How! - exclaimed the Master full of fervor. – But you were poor and humble with clean hands, and this seems to you as not being enough?! ...

- An inept. – mutters the Poverello, smiling weakly and low-spirited, - Why do you not say instead, that I took advantage of the charity of others in order not to die of hunger? - says two seconds later a little uplifted.

- Marvellous! Perfect! Exemplary! – sayd emphatically the Master, with his eyes looking at the sky and the arms rigid towards the ground.

- Rather comfortable and a little cowardly ...

- Ah, you should not downgrade yourself now?! – the Master says in a tone of reproach and a little offended.

- If I think about it, - says the Poverello with more strength, - deep down I am ashamed ... the charity creates a vicious circle, - he says looking at his Master with regret, - because the one who is doing charity to us, is convinced of booking a place in paradise, or at the least believes to cleanse his conscience! And we let him believe it! Is it true or not, that we let him believe it?! And in this way, I do not like this at all ... Do you not see that the matter assumes shady tones? Do you not see that it becomes moral extortion.

- But no, it is not so! – replies the Master unconvinced – Not even the charity now!? The charity had always done good!

- You know, one does not feel like working, and it becomes mystical to scrounge! - continues unabated the Poverello.

- But you are not one of those, you have not failed in anything.

- I have failed against my dignity, Master, and it does not seem just to me that there are two classes: that of those who work and that of the parasites.

- Parasite! - exclaimed the Master angry and red in the face, - I have preached poverty and more poverty! Because when there is money in question, inevitably there is corruption and rot.

- Perhaps in denouncing the corruption that comes from money, you are somewhat confused; one matter is poverty or rather the honesty or perhaps parity, another matter is to be the parasites.

- But better, - the Master shouts excitedly, - what more could there have been done?

- You, for example, what better could you do?

- Make me useful, truly useful in some way ... and above all to earn my bread, always by means of a vicious cycle! Men are not birds, if they do not sow and gather, they do not eat.

- Look! – says the Master visibly offended, - precisely from you comes the moral.

- Come on! - minimizes the Poverello with sweetness, - You were in good faith, only that you missed a bit of sense of reality. The manna does not fall from the clouds! You see, - continued calmly the Poverello, - I want to say that the mysticism is not and should not be a profession and cannot be acquired with a priest's cassock, and more less it should not be lived by a charity of others. Mysticism is the noblest part of man, and if is sacrilegious to offend or trade it. I mean to say that one who is equal to you would not dare ever to do charity! If anything, you can share with your equal and not throw the leftovers to a passing stray dog; you would think that perhaps it was a lack of respect, you would think of offending his dignity.

- Of course, - the Master says thoughtfully, - the noblest part of man cannot live by alms.

Scene N° 13

Rome: Colosseum 2013

The sphere of light is at the center of the Colosseum. The Man of Liberation continues to work on one side of the sphere. The Master and the Poverello are standing beside the base. The tribunes are crowded with people as if in transparency as ghosts of the thousands of crucified men who appear to be still alive and who complain and struggle. Their naked bodies are tortured and impaled by arrows. The sky seems as if painted dark red.

The Master kneels down on the ground and raises his hands up to the sky.

- What kind of madness are the martyrs! - cries the Master looking at crucifixes, - Why do you kill these poor wretched people?! - says almost crying, - To go where? To witness what? – the Master puts his head between the palms of his hands and weeps, then raises his head and looking at the crucifixes utters shouting: -

- Now, it appears that I only function as a great political and economic empire. They do nothing for the souls.

- Please, do not fret, you do not need to agitate yourself. - says the moved Poverello.

- Then let me relieve myself! I have one of those needles here! – shouts louder the

Master, striking his chest with a fist - Look how is reduced my doctrine, look what I have died for, look what these idiots have died for!! The history of the Church, from the time it has had its power from the Roman Empire, is a story of continuous crimes and oppressions.

This story then continues with the most barbaric intolerance, expressed in the Crusades and in 500 years of inquisition, which resulted in hundreds of millions being murdered, in my name! I, - adds he with desolate expression and with tears and lump in his throat, - I, who had always preached tolerance and kindness.

The Curriculum Vitae of the Church is the most criminal in the human history! - he continues shouting louder and pointing to the crucifixes, - Anyone can commit any crime ... it is enough that one day one meets a priest, and can come out of it clean and white as a lily, and every time like this, I am so good! I died on purpose! It is enough to re-enter the sheep's fold, you do not need anything else ... when you wish, you enter;

they say it is enough just to repent, even at the time of death. In this way, though, - says the Master with bitterness, - you do not have the men behind you, but only pigs and sheep!

- You have done well your part of the messiah. - says the Man of Liberation.

- In my days, there was a sense, - says the Master in desolation, - but now?

- If it were not for you, perhaps there would have been another! Maybe worse than you! Maybe it was an inevitable historic event. - says the man as if to comfort him.

The Master is still on his knees on the ground. The Man of Liberation, who was suspended in mid-air, is standing next to him. After a few seconds...

- And then – continues the Master, - perhaps they count the words? Vain and chimerical words! Whatever a Master says, is always misunderstood, is manipulated or duped! ...

The Master looks at the crucifixes with infinite pity, some of them have already expired.

- I too, when I see clear .. have already pictured what they would build behind my back; I was about to die when I saw it all clear! What could I have done then? ... What can I do now? - after a few seconds of silence continues with more strength,

- A man can express his ideas, his thoughts, I do not deny it, but in a responsible way! ... Some nonsense cannot be repeated eternally in the centuries! They have loaded me in one mode! That it will be difficult to find in books one who is more megalomaniac than I appear to be. ... I, - says he with anguish, I was dying in despair! Torturing myself like a fool, covered mainly in unhappiness! - I too, died for nothing! How to remedy it now?! How?! - asks the Master even more prostrated.

Scene N°14

At the foot of the luminous sphere over the hill.

- Look. - says the Master turning to the Man of Liberation, - When you believe to be God, inevitably one always exaggerates a little.

- I think that the man had created a God, above all in order to make a receptacle for all his unconscious fears. - says the man calmly without being distracted from his work.

- Ah, of course, - says the Master with emphasis - and have built Churches, Cathedrals, Abbeys and golden altars - full is the earth - but now a man has less fear, and by losing the fear has lost its spirituality and the sacred meaning of life; today a man does not believe in anything, he has no longer the values! .. He is just a piece of flesh that heads towards self-destruction. Who knows, if he could still believe in something.

After few seconds of silence, the Master says with desolation: - I also do not believe in anything. - and facing the Man of Liberation cries out: -

- In what do you believe in?

The Man of Liberation responds calmly: -

- I believe in reality, existence, the essence of my being, in the nature, eternal and infinite universe and in all that surrounds me, and that this reality is free from cause or supernatural intervention. And I believe it all with great love.

- Well, deep down you are not wrong. I likewise, if I was of the present time, I would believe what you believe. Yes, - the Master says deep in thought, - of course! ... at least ... at least I believe, of course I do! - after a couple of seconds: - I wanted to save the man! - He says impetuously, - I blindly believed in my mission, but sometimes we confuse ourselves! Now that a two thousand years had passed, I say that too often the good faith is nothing more than an excuse to clean the conscience! Even with the good faith one can kill in an error, thousand of millions could be killed! One can do wars and genocides, in good faith! And not only material, but also moral and spiritual. How many wars, how many genocides, how many have been murdered in my name in these two millenniums! How many, - yells in anger - one million, ten million, a hundred million! How many!

The Master throws himself on the ground like in the throes of an epileptic seizure, and when the crisis was over he was completely exhausted, burying his face in the grass with the body all stiffened. Christiana, alarmed, goes to rescue him, placing his head between the palms of her hands, as in a modern piety. The Poverello, in a state of panic, approaches the Master and trembling like a leaf takes his hands.

After few moments, the Master regains consciousness and opens his eyes.

- How do you feel? – enquires the Poverello.

- I feel good, I feel good. – responds the Master sitting up and running a hand over his head.

- You know that it hurts you when you get angry? – says the Poverello.

- It is nothing, it is nothing. - Master says, with his face contorted – It is that I have seen too much around! I am like a puppet in the hands of madness. And all those masses which have been frustrated ever since, the same ones that I wanted to redeem. The right way to liberty always passes from under their noses, perhaps it is because they do not even know what it is. As long as they are repressed, manoeuvred and marked from conception. And precisely those masses are still licking their lips over a dish stale and mouldy, which stinks from what has gone bad, but which is so skillfully packaged as to be the only choice within their reach. And what is worse, is that they believe that they are choosing it.

The Master is silent for a while, but is restless. He runs a hand on his cheek, then on the beard, then under the chin. Finally, he clears up his voice and looking at the Man of Liberation, says with a little uncertainty:-

- You sit here all alone! What a desert, as there is nobody here? For whom do you work?

- Perhaps the flock is lost. - says the man smiling.

- But perhaps instead they have lost track of the path. - resumed the Master excitedly, - Myself, I have barely glimpsed at them. I have sown over the grass so thick and durable.

- I think, - says the Man of Liberation - that the great difficulty of the masses is to accept the loneliness of their being, - and blowing off the dark red dust from the Sphere, continues always calmly – they prefer to believe that they form a part of the great and mysterious, elusive plan of the divine nature. In the end, this is a fixed idea, that somewhere there is a master – a father. They feel reassured to think about that.

- Why do you think that we think? - asks the Master with an ironic smile, - Who knows what those have in mind! Not of course the loneliness of being! Those do not know that the brain serves to think! And then let us assume that they do know, in any case what do they do? - continues the irate Master, - They refuse any liability to the primary reasons of existence, denying any mental disposition. They do not know how to administer it all by themselves, and then to what freedom they pretend to? They are always in need of halters. But, - he says regretfully, - the human idiocy is one thing that never ceases to surprise me! A man has always fought to free himself from slavery and masters, and holds tight to himself what he teaches to others.

The Master looks up at the Man of Liberation and says: -

- At least in the mythology there was some form of democracy of the deity, but after my event a dictatorial fact has occurred which had developed a severe state of spiritual and intellectual repression in a man! .. You, for example, are working on the Liberation and I do not see a dog around! ... I do not understand why you do it; the fact is that I am here deliberately for you ... I do not know. - the Master says, underlining his words, - You appear to me as the right man .. You look a suitable man indeed. - says cautiously peering the other to grasp any reaction, but nothing happens. The Man of Liberation says nothing. Christiana too looks at the man and expects a reaction, but nothing comes forth.

- Well! - Master says, - I think you are suitable enough to take out the chestnuts from the fire for me! Otherwise, damn, what are you doing here?! – shouts the Master angrily.

- Instead, I think that we are alone with ourselves in the eternal infinity, - says finally the man, - and that on the threshold of the perfect nothing are deflagrated each of our alternations, because the reality is in the order of all things, and makes part of us. We recognize ourselves in our individual entity, as the mind of the universe, a mind that aspires to eternal love and universal beauty. This we may be, we can do this.

- Ah! You are too quiet, my dear, too closed within yourself! Damn, you have to move! The idealists have to be in a hurry, have more passion. You are too silent! You talk too little! - says the Master exasperated, collecting the pebbles from the ground and throwing them away.

- Every philosophical thought precedes its historical moment. - says the man calmly.

- The things ought to be told clearly! Shouted in a loud voice, engaging the crowds! Upsetting everything! Making a revolution, above all against those who have used my words, for their devious purposes of power over man.

- Make a war? - asks the man.

- Of course! And what with that? - urges the Master increasingly stubborn and white from rage, - Perhaps not in my name they have fought, killed and vulgarly plundered to widen the frontiers of their empire? ... I have been besmirched! Do you not understand?

Never, I say, never! Human dignity was raped and mortified in this way, and with this? You make lots of problems, many scruples; well, you can too fight you war, can't you! Amen, ... if there will be casualties, at least this time will be the right occasion!

- I do not want to do a part of a teacher, nor a messiah. - replies the Man of Liberation, cool-headed and composed, stopping for a moment his work, – I am not here to preach or convert, - then adds, - because assuming that the truth is white: contrary to this, the popularity is definitely black, and in practice the result will be even more gray, misrepresented and amorphous.

- But here we must prevail, one must do something! – says the Master not at all convinced, throwing over the shoulder the edge of his coat.

- What is the point? - says the man, - What would I do with millions of sheep that would follow me passively or actively, in an exactly the same manner as yesterday they followed a different shepherd?

- So, you do not give me any hope! – cries harshly the Master.

- Here is the point where the doctrines fail! - says the man, all serious, - The truth is not like a grain that is thrown to the hens! And the land - of a man, that he must conceive alone.

- In this way, we are unable to move forward! Ah, we are indeed not in a good shape! – says the Master with irony. - You are a poor deluded chap, if you think that things will change by themselves!

- Not the things, ourselves! - says the Man of Liberation, - Our conception of matters... On the other hand, any radical change needs its time, evolution itself requires it. Needless to force it.

- But you, what kind of ideals do you pursue in this way?

- I follow mine .. Every man will be a

philosopher and master of himself.

- Imagine that, - exclaims the Master, laughing ironically, - you do not know the men at all then! It takes a strong wrist, my dear fellow, the path ought to be shown in length and breadth, and if it is not enough, then take and place them on the road, otherwise they shall never arrive! You really have no idea how is made the entire humanity; it is like for some women for whom the meaning of freedom signifies prostituting!

- What do you search for? - says the man, - You want and do not want! In my opinion, you are only interested to change what is on the throne!

- And what if it is?!! – replies the Master with firmness, - I offer you the chance! - the two are looking deeply into each other's eyes; the man has a steady gaze and fixes on the eyes of the Master in a tone of reproach; the look of the Master challenges him for a couple of seconds, then giving in and in a tone of sorrow with a lump in the throat, he screams: - "At least look around! Have you looked around? Rages a horrendous decadence, what will happen...? They have no ideals, their fetishes are vanity, money and sex, and their human values have reached the point of Sodom and Gomorrah. Do you see that it takes a true leader, one of those who is able to break through these horizons which are so poor and deprived of meaning! ... Why do not you do something?!

- Make a new religion? - asks the man, - Again altars? Yours is the ancient evil!

- And you have too much faith in humanity!

- Maybe there will be a catharsis, the entire revolution. - says the man with a tranquil and still voice, motionless at the background of the Liberation.

- But you do not have any love for your own self? - screams the angry Master, - Meanwhile, I would not lift up a finger?

- Enough of the golden calves! Enough of the puppeteers who maneuver the spirituality of man!... We already live in all the disorder of the falling cathedrals.

- And meanwhile, here all is ruined, coward of a land! - shouts angrily the Master without any restraint, and beating his fists on the ground, cries:- "I am tired, do you understand? And I am tired a lot! Do you want to understand?!

- Perhaps the man will be re-born from this waste. - says the Man of Liberation, with a light tone of consolation.

The Master, full of bitterness and desolation, stands up and remains as if turned to stone with an absent look. The Poverello approaches him and with much grace and sweetness draws the Master to sit on the floor next to him, and rests the Master's head on his chest.

Christiana looks with worry at the Man of Liberation and says:

- To follow one's own belief might not be a convenient way to live in an internal anarchy, masking the indiscipline under the aegis of principle?

- You see, - utters calmly the Man of Liberation, - a man cannot cheat himself, there, with his naked soul in front of him .... Who takes the commitment to an inner search, personal and detailed on the fundamental issues of existence, I do not think that he or she do it for forging a cover for his or her small, cowardly and mediocre personal interests.

- You believe so? - asks Christiana.

- The poor sinners, those who follow a doctrine half way, often indulging in a succulent evasion, believe that it is only a cover.

- To those who seek alone, this cannot happen?

- If you did all this just to throw the smoke in the eyes, you would be a fool! It would have been enough just to exit from the ranks of the flock and re-enter at the right appropriate moment ... each time the circumstances require, or perhaps only to obtain the forgiveness in the end .. They are all like that. They believe that they fear God and imbued with good feelings! .. instead they are just a shapeless mass, apathetic in reality, in constant expectation of resolutions, blind and groping!

- Why are you here? The man asks.

- I do not know where to go, humanity is seriously ill, cathedrals have fallen down. – responds Christiana, feeling desolate.

- Can you see the Liberation? Now my work is accomplished.

- I only see a bank of luminous fog. - says Christiana.

The man comes close to her and cuts loose from the body the strings of a puppet. While he loosens the strings, Christiana sees the fog dissolving; her face illuminates with light and an ecstatic astonishment.

- Now I see it! I see it! – exclaims she beaming. - I see all the infinite Universe. I see and hear all the Truth and Knowledge. I see and hear Love, all the Art and Poetry. I hear the most sublime Music, and I feel a part of Everything.

The Master and the Poverello turn to look at the sphere that pulsates with light. A few moments later, the Master looks at the man and recognizes in the face of the man, himself.

Pulsating, the sphere of light grows bigger and bigger, absorbing in itself everyone.

The End.

Biographical Notes on the life of Denis Diderot

Denis Diderot was born on the 5th of October 1713 in Langres, a small town in the Champagne region, 250km from Paris and 160km from Reims. His father Didier was a craftsman cutler, also a manufacturer of excellent surgical instruments, who continued the centenary family tradition of this work. His mother was Angélique Vérignon, a daughter of merchants and tanners of ancient times.

The Diderot and The Vérignon families were both wealthy, very Catholic and tradition-bound, and there were many abbots and nuns counted among their ancestors. The little Diderot grew up with this type of education and at the age of ten years old he attended the Jesuits College in Langres, with much profit, regarding which he wrote the following:- "I sucked the milk of Homer, Virgil, Horace, Terence, Anacreon, Plato and Euripides, diluted with that of Moses and other Prophets of the Bible."

His studies continued at the Colleges of the Jesuits and Louis le Grand in Paris, and thereafter in 1732, he graduated from the University of Paris as the"Maitre dès Arts" (Master of Arts).

Against the will of his patriarch father Didier,

who wished for his son a serious profession, Diderot answered vaguely not knowing what to do, meanwhile giving lessons in mathematics, even if his passion for theatre was pressing him toward a career of an actor; he also meditated to be an abbot.

Only the passion for the beauty of his future wife, Annette-Toinette Champion, lead him to see himself clearly, and to prefer the mental inclination of the Nature to those of clerical education which he had received.

As happens to certain exceptional and creative intellectuals, where the strong individuality is confronted with the conformist world of social tradition ruled by religion, that they find - precisely in that religious education - the elements of greater critical comparison with regard to the natural and rational world of the Reason; as had happened before Diderot to Giordano Bruno and thereafter to Nietzsche.

In 1742, Diderot translates from the English language: Grecian History written by Temple Stanyan, upon which evidence of work he relied a lot in convincing his father to give his consent and economic means necessary to marry Annette-Toinette Champion. His father – being contrary to the marriage, threatened Diderot that he would disinherit him if he did not keep the promise to become an abbot, and by force locks Diderot up in the convent of the monks. Diderot escaped from a window and with fatigue reached Paris. Shortly thereafter, he married Annette and had the first daughter Angélique, who bore the same name as his mother and his sister nun.

Diderot undertook an activity as a translator, acquainting with the English philosophers such as: Francis Bacon, Isaak Newton and John Loke, and it will be precisely these philosophers to introduce him in the rational world of logic and reason, and the scientific interpretation of natural phenomena, as already these philosophers had influenced Voltaire. Even if it must be said that the influence of the English philosophers had an evolutionary development in the thought of the atheist Diderot, whereas it remained the same in the deist Voltaire.

In 1745, Diderot translated from English into French the work of Lord Shaftesbury: "An Essay on the Merit and Virtue". This work, with reflections of Diderot, was published in Paris, with no indication as to its author, and with false editorial indications, resulting to had been printed in Amsterdam. This contrivance was used to escape the censorship dominated by the clerical power, which was not content with just burning a book, but also emprisoned the writer.

From 1743 to 1745, Diderot translates from English into French, the Medical Dictionary by Robert James.

In 1746, he wrote his first work "Philosophical Thoughts", the book that forms part of the deist-atheist literature, and which was published clandestinely in 1756, and thereafter condemned to the fire by the Parliament of Paris.

In 1747, Diderot wrote "The Walk of the Skeptic", with definitely atheistic reflections therein, where the free-thinkers are placed in a tranquil avenue of chestnut trees, while the religious men are in the avenue of thorns.

In the month of October, the bookseller and printer Le Breton entrusts to Diderot and d'Alembert the directorial role of the Encyclopaedia, a much broader and richer work than that published in London in 1728, which from the initial project had to be only translated from English into French.

The Encyclopaedia, according to Diderot, had to have a new conception of the world, as opposed to the metaphysical and theological idea, liberating the human-being from the religious imbroglio, the common thinking.

Diderot had been committed to this work of social renewal from 1746 to 1772, while d'Alembert - for economic contrasts with Le Breton - had abandoned the Encyclopaedia seven years prior to its completion.

Diderot, being very bitter and disappointed on how his Encyclopaedia was treated, wrote to Catherine II of Russia: "I have worked almost thirty years on this work. Of all the persecutions that one can imagine, there does not exist not even one that I have not endured. I risked losing my honor, my wealth and freedom. My manuscripts circulated hidden from one place to another, and they have tried several times to withhold them. I spent sleepless nights with the danger of being imprisoned. My friends were advising me to leave the country. The Encyclopaedia was proscribed and I, myself was threatened in person by various edicts of the King as well as various decrees of the Parliament.

My enemies have been the court, the clergy, the police and the judiciary authorities, together with all the people influenced by the power.

One infamous publisher has mutilated ten volumes and burned the manuscripts.".

Diderot attempted to propose to Catherine II, to work for a few years with his collaborators, in order to publish the uncensored Encyclopaedia, but, unfortunately, Catherine II did not satisfy his request.

It is truly paradoxical that *"Encyclopédie"*, which is the most representative work of the European Enlightenment, is actually the most mutilated and censored work, very far from how Diderot had wished for it to appear.

In 1749, Diderot clandestinely prints the "A Letter on Blindness for the use of those who have their sight."

In this essay Denis Diderot develops a materialist theory in oppositioin to the theory of the divine creation of the world. In this way, there developes an evolutionary theory of continuous transformation of the matter, which anticipates Charles Darwin. Denis Diderot sends to Voltaire the "Letter on Blindness for the use of those who have their sight.", and on this occasion there commences the friendly relationship between the two writers, even if the deist Voltaire criticizes the atheist tendency of the essay.

On 24th of July of even year, immediately

after a search of his home by the police, Diderot was arrested and imprisoned in the dungeon of Vincennes. Interrogated, Diderot denies being the author of the the work "A Letter on Blindness for the use of those who have their sight.", but then confesses and promisses not to write again matters contrary to religion. Under the pressure by the encyclopaedia publishers to the authorities, Diderot was released in November of the same year.

Meanwhile, the detention in the prison of Vincennes earned him fame, even if Diderot remained very much tried by the bad experience.

In June of 1751, a first volume of Encyclopaedia was released, despite of it being heavily censored; the Jesuits attacked the work and accused Diderot and d'Alembert of having followed the scientific and rational system of Francis Bacon, favoring the religion of Nature as opposed to the revealed dogmatic Christian religion. The Jesuits managed to prohibit, by a royal decree, the sale and publication of this work.

The desperate editors influenced Madame de Pompadour on the cultural values of Encyclopaedia, and luckily in the meantime, the Jesuits came into contrast with the regal power. Thus, the publishers obtained a permission for publication and the continuance of this work, provided that there was no mention of religion or political power therein. To guarantee these conditions, three theological censors were entrusted to carry out the revisions of the manuscript drafts. Despite these censors, Diderot made all possible to ensure that the Encyclopaedia retained its identity.

In 1752, Diderot clandestinely and anonymously published the *"Thoughts on the Interpretation of Nature"*.

An essay that honors the scientific method of searching for truth of things, in line with the Novum Organum of Francis Bacon.

In 1755, Diderot began his love affair with the woman of his life, Sophie Volland, who was very different from his wife Anne-

Toinette Champion, for whom were more important the practical things of everyday life and material well-being, than the ideals of her husband.

Sophie Volland was very important for the life of Diderot, because in her he has not only found a true love and the deep meaning of this feeling, but also a confidant friend that gave him the feeling of safety and well-being, together with a profound meaning to his life, as is evidenced from the rich correspondence which passed between them for over 20 years.

In 1757, after the release of the sixth volume of the *"Encyclopaedia"*, Diderot - who has never lost his keen interest in the theatre - published: "An Illegitimate Son", and a year later: "The Father of the Family". The theatre of Diderot is founded on the primary value of the individual, regardless if one has had aristocrats or bourgeois origins. In this, is outlined the quality of the democratic ideal, as opposed to those of the aristocracy of his time.

The year of 1759 was the year of great crisis for the *"Encyclopaedia"*. After the publication of the essay: "On the Spirit" by Helvetius, a decidedly materialistic work, the clergy with the government - considering it sacrilegious - wanted to combine and give the responsibility of the essay of Helvetius to the main director of the *"Encyclopaedia"* - Diderot, considering the work to be blasphemous and condemning it to be burned.

Even the Pope Clement XIII, condemned the *"Encyclopaedia"*, exhorting the faithful believers - who might have been in possession of the volumes of this work - to deliver these volumes to the local bishops, so that they could burn them without delay.

After these facts as well as the economic contrasts with publishers, d'Alembert - the main and valuable collaborator of Diderot – withdrew himself from the direction of the *"Encyclopaedia"*. Diderot was left alone to conduct the immense work which he continued doing in hiding, fighting fearlessly against the obscurantism of power.

In 1760, Diderot writes: *"The Nun"*, which deals with a report against the religious communities of the convents, where the pretentious unnatural life of "holiness", the inherent withdrawal from the evil of the world, instead produces a world of sexual perversion and cruelty without equal, which characterise the author of these doings who also becomes the victim of evil.

It is worth noting that Diderot's sister Angélique, died in a convent having become insane.

The convent also became a way of burying alive the women of noble families, who did not want to affect their assets with costly dowry which they had to give to their daughters to find husbands of the same rank. Or, as in the case of the protagonist of the novel Suzanne Simonin, to eliminate from society daughters born from adulterous relationships.

In 1761, Diderot commenced writing the satirical novel: *"Rameau's Nephew"*. In this novel, the nephew of a great musician invents ingenious stratagems to be able to be the most appreciable parasite, who flatters the vanity of the ruling class. Here, Diderot wants to denounce the decadence of the society of this time, where intelligence and creativity are humiliated, being at service of the bleak personal convenience.

The novel was finished in 1777, and the work was published in France only in 1823.

From 1765 to 1767, Diderot writes: *"Notes on Painting"*, which thereafter was published in the "Correspondance Littéraire" of his friend Grimm.

Diderot intends the art to be as a means of the evolution of society, where a reality is represented by holding present the universal values of man, to his or her progress of knowledge by means of the logic of the Reason, poetized and idealized by the sublimation of Nature and Life .

In 1769, Diderot undertakes to summarize his philosophy by writing: *"D'Alembert's*

Dream". By means of a dream of his friend, which is expressed in a clear rational materialism, Diderot wished to express the instinctive quality of his evolved mind, which interprets the Nature as a succession of vital processes, and which follow the chemical and physical rules, independent of any supernatural will.

In 1782, Diderot ends his work titled: "*An Essay on the Reign of Claudius and Nero*", where Diderot defends defamatory criticism of Seneca, who preferred to kill himself, rather than living the good life of corruption.

In 1783, dies his dear friend d'Alembert, and in February of 1784 also passes away his beloved Sophie Volland.

Diderot, who saw life as a wonderful dream of happiness, by means of Knowledge, and who perceived death as a tranquil process of Freedom which is necessary for the Eternity of Nature - will die himself without even noticing it, as writes his daughter Angélique: "Saturday, 31st of July 1784 ... sat at the table, ate some soup of boiled mutton and chicory; took an apricot that my mother wanted to prevent him from eating, when he said "What the devil, do you think it will do to me?". Having ate it, leaned his elbow on the table to eat the jam of cherries, coughed slightly. My mother asked him something and, since there was no answer from him, lifted his head to look at him: he was dead.

Milton Keynes UK
Ingram Content Group UK Ltd.
UKHW020829131124
2812UKWH00004B/7